Island

RETOLD BY PAULINE FRANCIS

EVANS BROTHERS LIMITED

Published by Evans Brothers Limited
2A Portman Mansions
Chiltern Street
London W1U 6NR

This Evans Centenary edition first published 2008

Printed in China by WKT Co. Ltd.

British Library Cataloguing in Publication data
Francis, Pauline
    Treasure Island. – Abridged ed. – (Fast track classics)
    1. Treasure Island (Imaginary place) – Juvenile fiction
    2. Pirates – Juvenile fiction 3. Adventure stories
    4. Children's stories
    I. Title II. Stevenson, Robert Louis, 1850–1894
    823.9'2 [J]

ISBN-13: 9780237535483

VISIT OUR WEBSITE
www.evansbooks.co.uk

Treasure Island

Introduction

Robert Louis Stevenson was born in 1850, in Edinburgh, Scotland. After studying law at Edinburgh University, he decided to earn his living as a writer. Unfortunately, he became ill with tuberculosis, a disease of the lungs, and he had to travel to warmer countries to improve his health. However, he did earn some money by writing about his travels.

In 1880, Robert Louis Stevenson married Fanny Osborne and, a year later, he wrote *Treasure Island* for her young son. In 1886, *Kidnapped* was published. Both these books were very popular, but they did not make much money. So, in 1886, Stevenson wrote *The Strange Case of Dr Jekyll and Mr Hyde.* This story made Stevenson well known, and made him more money, because it was bought by adults.

Treasure Island is an exciting adventure story in which a young boy, Jim Hawkins, tells us of his hunt for buried treasure and his fight with pirates led by the one-legged Long John Silver. It is still one of the best-loved stories for children.

In 1887, Stevenson's father died. With the money that he left, Robert Louis Stevenson and his family were able to live in Samoa, an island in the Pacific Ocean. The warm climate improved his health and he wrote there until his death in 1894.

My name is Jim Hawkins. My friends have asked me to write down my adventures, from beginning to end. I shall tell you the story of Treasure Island; but I shall not tell you where the island is, because there is still some treasure there.

Let me go back to the very beginning when I was living in Black Hill Cove, at the Admiral Benbow Inn. My father was the landlord there. One day, a sun-burned old seaman, with a scar across his cheek, knocked on our door. I remember him as if it were yesterday...

CHAPTER ONE

The black spot

I watched the old sailor from the window. He dragged a sea-chest to the door, looked out to sea for a while, then started to sing:

> "Fifteen men on the dead man's chest –
> Yo-ho-ho, and a bottle of rum!"

He rapped on the door with a piece of wood.

"Is it quiet here, mate?" he asked my father.

My father nodded.

"Well, then," the old man cried, "this is the ship for me! I'll stay here a bit. I'm a simple man – rum and bacon and eggs is all I want. You can call me captain."

He threw three or four gold coins onto the counter. And a few days later, he called me over to his seat in the window and held up a silver coin.

"Keep your eyes open, boy," he said, "for a sailor with one leg and I'll give you one of these on the first day of every month."

How I watched and waited for that one-legged man to come to the inn! He even began to haunt my dreams. On stormy nights, when the wind shook the house, and the waves roared, I would see him in my sleep. Sometimes, his leg would be cut off at the knee, sometimes at the hip. Sometimes he chased me over hedges and ditches. Yes, I earned my money well.

"That man will be the ruin of us," my father complained one day. "I have used up all his gold already. When I ask for more, he snorts like a fog-horn."

One bitterly cold January day, I was laying the table for the captain's breakfast when a tall stranger stepped into the room. Two fingers were missing from his left hand.

"Is this here table for my mate Bill?" he asked.

"I do not know your mate Bill," I replied.

"Well," he said, "my mate Bill would be called the captain. He has a long scar on his cheek…and a very pleasant manner when he's had a drink of rum."

He stared at me.

"Now, is my mate Bill here in this house?"

"He's out walking," I told him.

I hoped that the stranger would go away. But he waited by the inn door, peering round the corner like a cat waiting for a mouse. At last, the captain came in, and, without looking to the right or left, walked straight to his table.

"Bill," boomed the stranger.

The captain spun round. The colour drained from his face, and even his nose was blue. He looked like a man who had seen a ghost.

"Black Dog!" he gasped.

"We'll sit down, if you like," said Black Dog, "and talk like old shipmates."

I left them drinking rum. They mumbled and muttered for a long time. Then they began to swear at each other. I heard the crash of the table and chairs, followed by a cry of pain.

I went to see what was happening. Black Dog was running away from the captain, blood flowing from his shoulder. The captain raised his sword and would have killed Black Dog; but his sword stuck in the inn sign. You can still see the mark today.

Black Dog disappeared over the hill and the captain fell to the floor, unconscious. My poor father was also ill at this time and Doctor Livesey came to see them both.

When the captain opened his eyes, I took him some food and drink. He seemed very excited.

"I've seen old Flint there in the corner," he told me.

He caught hold of my arm.

"I was on Captain Flint's ship once," he said weakly, "I'm the only man who knows the place, Jim."

"The doctor says you're to stay in bed a week," I told him briskly.

"If they send me the black spot, it's the sea-chest they're after," he gasped. "If they come, get on your horse, Jim, and tell that doctor friend to fetch help and round up all Flint's old crew…especially the man with one leg – him above all, Jim."

"But what is the black spot, captain?" I asked.

"It's an order," he whispered, "an order that has to be obeyed."

And he fell asleep.

I would have gone to the doctor straight away, but my

father died suddenly that evening. The day after his funeral, about three o' clock on a foggy, frosty afternoon, I was standing by the door, staring sadly out to sea. The sound of tapping made me look up.

I had never seen such a terrifying man.

He was hunched over inside a huge old sea-cloak. He was blind and wore a great green eye shade over his eyes and nose. The horrible, eyeless creature gripped my hand tightly.

"Now, take me to the captain," he said.

"Sir," I replied, "I dare not. He is very ill."

"Take me, boy, or I'll break your arm," he said.

I never heard a voice so cruel, so cold and so ugly. I led him over to the captain at once. He looked sick with terror as we came in.

"Now, Bill, sit where you are," said the blind man, "and hold out your left hand. Boy, take his left hand by the wrist and bring it near to my right."

We both obeyed. I saw the blind man pass something from his hand into the palm of the captain's hand. Then, he suddenly left us. The captain looked down at his hand.

"Ten o'clock!" he cried.

Then he fell to the floor quite dead. I knelt down beside him. On the floor, close to his hand, was a little round piece of paper. It was blackened on one side.

"The black spot!" I gasped.

CHAPTER TWO

Escape from the inn

I turned the paper over and read the message on it.

"You have till ten tonight."

The clock started to chime, and I almost jumped out of my skin; but it was only six o'clock. I went to fetch my mother.

"Now, Jim," she said, locking the door, "where's the key to the captain's sea-chest? I want the money he owes me."

I felt in the captain's pockets, then opened his shirt at the neck. There it was, hanging on a piece of string. We hurried up to his room and unlocked the sea-chest.

"A good suit!" she exclaimed, "some shells and… here we are, Jim, his money-bag!"

She started to count out some gold coins. Suddenly, I put my hand on her arm. In the silent, frosty air I could hear the tap-tapping of a stick on the frozen road. It came nearer and nearer. The stick struck the inn door. The handle turned and the bolt rattled. Then we heard the tapping move away. We were terrified.

"I'll take what I have counted so far," said my mother.

I caught sight of an envelope wrapped in oil-skin.

"And I'll take this instead of the rest of the money!" I cried.

We ran out of the inn. We had not started a minute too soon. The fog was beginning to lift and the moon shone on men running with lanterns towards us. We hid under a bridge.

I was soon more curious than afraid. I left my mother and crept towards the inn where I hid behind a bush. Seven or eight men were running towards the door, two of them leading the blind man. They broke down the door and I could hear their feet rattling up our old stairs. Then someone threw open the window of the captain's room.

"They've been before us," he shouted. "Bill's dead, but the money's here."

"Is *it* there?" asked the blind man.

"We don't see it nowhere," the man replied.

"It's that boy! I wish I had put his eyes out!" he shouted back. "Scatter, lads! You'll be as rich as kings if you can find it."

They smashed everything inside our inn. Then, furious, they began to quarrel among themselves. In this way, they lost time and did not see the policemen galloping so fast down the hill that their horses knocked the blind man to the ground, stone dead.

"I must find a safe place for the captain's envelope," I told myself. "I'll go to Doctor Livesey. He'll know what to do."

I left my poor mother at a friend's house and set off to see the doctor. But he was dining with Mr. Trelawney, the squire who owned most of the land in the village. I ran all the way to the squire's house and made them listen to my story.

"Have you heard of this Captain Flint?" the doctor asked Mr. Trelawney.

"Heard of him!" he cried. "Heard of him, you say! He was the bloodthirstiest pirate that ever sailed the sea."

"If *I* tell you that I might know where Flint buried some of his treasure?" asked the doctor, "will that treasure be worth very much?"

"Very much?" roared the squire, "enough for me to want to get a ship ready now, and take you and Hawkins along. I'll have that treasure if I search a year."

"Very well," said the doctor. "Now, then, if Jim agrees, we'll open Flint's envelope."

I nodded and the doctor cut the stitches holding the oil-skin together. Inside was a sealed paper. The doctor opened the seals carefully and out fell a map of an island.

We all stared at it. The island was about nine miles long and five miles wide, like a fat dragon standing up. It had two fine harbours and a hill in the centre marked *"The Spy-Glass"*. We could see three crosses of red ink, two on the north part of the island, one in the south-west. Next to this last cross were the words *"Most of treasure here."*

I turned the map over and found these words:

> *"Tall tree, Spy-glass shoulder,*
> *compass point N. of NNE.*
> *Skeleton Island ESE and by E*
> *Ten feet."*

The squire kept his word. A few weeks later, the three of us sailed for Treasure Island.

CHAPTER THREE

Long John Silver

We sailed on the *Hispaniola* with Captain Smollett and eighteen seamen. When I first met the cook, Long John Silver, I almost jumped out of my skin. His leg had been cut off at the hip! Was he the one-legged pirate I had looked out for at the inn?

I watched him all the time; but I liked what I saw. He was clean and tidy and friendly. He worked cheerfully, hanging his wooden crutch around his neck when he was cooking.

"No, he *can't* be a pirate," I said to myself.

Long John Silver also took a liking to me.

"Sit you down, Jim," he used to say, "and have a talk."

Then he would point to his parrot.

"I calls my parrot Cap'n Flint, after the famous pirate," he told me.

"Pieces of eight! Pieces of eight! Pieces of eight! Pieces of eight! Pie…" the bird squawked.

Silver threw his handkerchief over the parrot's cage to quieten him.

"What does he mean, pieces of eight?" I asked.

"Why, they're gold coins," laughed Silver, "taken from

sunken Spanish ships."

How wrong I was about John Silver! One evening, just after sunset, I decided to fetch an apple from the barrel on deck. There were very few apples left and I had to climb inside. It was warm and dark in there and I almost fell asleep. Suddenly, I heard Silver talking to Israel Hands, the man who steered the ship.

"Here's what I want to know, Barbecue," said Israel Hands, "how long are we going to wait?"

"Till *I* give the word," Silver replied. "This squire and doctor shall find the treasure, and help us to get it aboard. *Then* we'll kill them."

I was terrified. I realised that the lives of all the honest men on board depended on me alone. Silver and Hands sent for some rum.

"Here's to old Flint!" they cried.

And almost at the same time, a voice from the mast-top called out: "Land ho!" and everyone ran up to the deck as the captain gave his orders. I slipped out of the barrel and ran to find Doctor Livesey.

"Doctor, call the captain and squire down to the cabin. I have terrible news for you," I whispered.

He did as I asked and I told the three of them what I had just overheard.

"So that's why Silver chose most of the men himself," sighed Captain Smollett. "Well, gentlemen, we must go on because we can't turn back. I think there are only seven honest men on board, including Jim. There might be nineteen men against us. We must wait."

In the morning, the sun was bright and hot and birds were diving for fish around us. We put down our anchor between Treasure Island and a small island called Skeleton Island. I should have been pleased to see land; but my heart sank into my boots. From my very first look, I hated Treasure Island.

The captain was worried.

"There's trouble in the air already," he told us. "I shall give the men time on shore with Silver. They will go with him. The rest of us will stay here, armed, and take the ship."

"I don't want to stay here," I thought, "I want to know what's going to happen."

I jumped into one of the boats and hid. When the boat came near the shore, I caught a branch over my head and swung out of the boat into the bushes. Silver and the men were still a hundred yards behind me. I ran until I found myself on an open piece of sandy land, dotted with pale, twisted trees.

For the first time in my life, I enjoyed exploring. I saw a snake high on a rock. As I passed by, it raised its head and hissed at me; but I did not know then how dangerous it was. Ahead, I could see the outline of

Spy-Glass Hill.

Suddenly, I heard a voice. I crept to the nearest tree and crouched there, as silent as a mouse. It was Silver and one of the seamen called Tom. I crawled nearer until I could hear what they were saying.

Then I heard another noise. It came from across the marsh — a sound like a cry of anger at first, then it became a long, long scream. The rocks of the Spy-Glass Hill echoed it and the marsh birds rose dark into the sky as the death-yell rang in my head.

Silver did not blink an eye at the sound. He did not make a move. He watched Tom like a snake about to spring.

"In heaven's name, Silver, tell me what was that?" Tom asked.

"That?" asked Silver, smiling and his face shining like glass. "That? Oh, that'll be Alan."

"Alan?" cried poor Tom. "You're no mate of mine now, John Silver. You've killed Alan, have you? Kill me, too, if you can."

And with these words, the brave Tom turned his back on Silver and walked towards the beach. With a cry, John Silver held onto the branch of a tree and hurled his crutch through the air. It struck poor Tom right between his shoulders, and he fell. He had no time to get up. As quick as a monkey, even without his crutch, Silver was on

top of him and twice buried his knife into Tom's body.

Silver and the birds, and the tall Spy-Glass Hill spun round and round before my eyes and I fainted. When I opened my eyes again, the monster was wiping his knife on the grass. Then he took a whistle from his pocket and blew it hard.

I was afraid for my life now.

"It is all over for me," I thought. "Goodbye to the *Hispaniola*; goodbye to the squire, the doctor and the captain!"

I ran like the wind until I came to a stony, steep hill with two peaks, scattered with pine trees. Suddenly, a stone came loose on the hill and rolled down between the trees. I saw a figure leap quickly behind a tree. Was it a bear? Was it a monkey? Or was it a man?

I could not tell. I froze on the spot with fear.

CHAPTER FOUR

The man of the island

There are murderers behind me and a murderer in front of me," I gasped. "Well, I prefer the danger I know."

With this thought, I began to run back towards the *Hispaniola*. Almost at once, the creature left his tree and tried to cut me off. He ran as fast as a deer, although he only had two legs. He was unlike any man I had ever seen.

I stood still for a moment. Then I remembered my pistol. This gave me the courage to walk towards the man.

"Who are you?" I asked.

To my surprise, the man threw himself to his knees.

"Ben Gunn," he answered in a husky voice. "I'm poor Ben Gunn, I am, and I haven't spoken to a man for three years."

Now I could see that he was pale skinned, although his lips were burned black by the sun. He wore clothes made from a ship's sail.

"Three years!" I cried. "Were you shipwrecked?" I asked.

"No, mate," he answered, "my captain left me here."
He stared at me.

"Now, you – what do you call yourself, mate?"

"Jim," I told him.

"Well, Jim," he whispered, "I'm rich."

He suddenly gripped my hand.

"Now, Jim, you tell me true. That ain't Flint's ship down there, is it?"

"No, Flint is dead," I said. "But there are some of Flint's old mates aboard, worse luck."

"Not a man – with one – leg?" he gasped.

"Silver?" I asked.

"Ah, Silver!" he said, "that were his name."

"He's the cook, and the ringleader too," I said.

I told him about the mutiny on board our ship.

"You just put your trust in Ben Gunn," he said. "Would your squire give me a passage home, Jim?"

I nodded.

"I'll tell you so much and no more," said Ben Gunn. "I were in the *Walrus,* Flint's ship, along with John Silver and Bill, when he buried the treasure. He took six men with him to dig, and he came back alone. Flint murdered them *all.* Well, three years ago, I were in another ship, and we sighted this island. I told my captain about the buried treasure. We landed and dug for twelve days; but we couldn't find it. The captain was so angry that he left me here to carry on digging. Now you go and tell the squire."

"How am I going to get back to the ship?" I asked.

"Well," he said, "I have my boat. I made it with my two hands. I keep her under the white rock."

He turned round.

"What's that?" he asked.

The sound of a cannon gun rang through the evening air.

"They have begun to fight!" I shouted. "Follow me!"

We ran towards the beach. I heard pistol shots. Then, over the top of the trees in front of me, I saw a Union Jack flag flying.

"There's your friends," Ben Gunn said.

"More likely it's the mutineers," I replied.

"No!" Gunn replied, "they would fly the Jolly Roger. Now I'm going. And when you've spoken to your squire, you can find me where you found me today. And, Jim, if you was to see Silver, you wouldn't tell him about Ben Gunn, will you?"

Before I could reply, a cannon ball came tearing through the trees and fell into the sands not far from where we were talking. I ran in one direction, Ben Gunn ran in another. The fighting carried on for more than an hour. I grew tired of waiting. The sun had just set and there was a gentle breeze. I could see the *Hispaniola* in the distance.

And from her mast flew a black pirate flag

25

CHAPTER FIVE

The white flag

I ran towards the woods in the direction of the Union Jack, where I hoped to find the squire and the doctor, if not all the other men who had stayed on the ship. In the distance, I saw a tall white rock.

"Is that where Ben Gunn keeps his boat?" I asked myself.

I came across an old log-cabin on a hill, surrounded by a circle of wooden posts. It was an old pirate stockade! But a sorry sight met my eyes. A dead body lay on the fence. But, to my relief, I found the doctor, the captain and the squire, and two other men safe and well inside the cabin.

"Jim!" cried the doctor, "I was worried for your safety. You should have stayed with us."

"What happened?" I asked. "Tell me what happened."

"We came ashore after you left," he said. "We were sick of waiting for trouble to start."

"How did you find this place?" I asked.

"It was on the map," said the doctor. "We went back to the ship several times to fetch food and gunpowder. I ordered the men left on the ship to follow me, but they refused. Israel Hands shot at us as we left, and sank our boat."

"The scoundrel!" I gasped.

"We carried everything here as best we could," he carried on, "but we lost some of our guns."

He looked at me and shivered.

"Then we heard that terrible scream, Jim. We thought *you* were dead."

We heard the pirates roaring and singing late into the night as we talked. I was so tired that when I got to sleep, I slept like a log, until a loud voice woke me up.

"White flag! White flag!" a man shouted.

I rushed to a spy hole and peeped out.

"It's Silver!" shouted the squire.

Sure enough, there were two men outside the stockade. One of them was waving a white cloth, and the other, John Silver himself, stood quietly at his side.

"Keep inside, men," said the captain, "this is a trick."

"Who goes? Stand, or we fire," shouted Captain Smollett.

"We want to talk," said Silver.

"Captain Silver, sir, wants to discuss peace," the other pirate said.

"*Captain* Silver! Don't know *him*. Who's he?" cried the captain.

Long John began to speak for himself.

"Me, sir," he said. "These poor lads have chosen me captain, after you *deserted*, sir."

"My man," laughed Captain Smollett, "I have *no* wish to talk to you. But if you wish to talk to me…"

Before he could finish, Long John Silver came over to the stockade, threw over his crutch, and climbed over the fence.

CHAPTER SIX
The battle begins

I was so surprised that I left my look-out post and went to sit behind the captain at the top of the steep slope. Silver had terrible trouble getting up there. In the soft sand, his crutch was of no use. But he got there in the end.

"Well?" asked Captain Smollett, coldly.

"Well, here it is, sir," said Silver. "We want that treasure, and we'll have it. You could save your lives. You have a map, haven't you"

"Possibly," said the captain.

"You have, I know that," said Silver. "What I mean is, we want your map. You give it to us and we'll offer you a choice. *Either* you come aboard ship with us when we've got the treasure. We'll share it, half each, and we'll take you safely wherever you want to go. *Or*, we'll share the treasure and I'll send a ship to pick you up."

"Is that all?" asked Captain Smollett.

"Every last word, by thunder!" answered Long John. "Refuse that and we'll fight you."

"Go!" said the captain.

"Give me a hand up!" cried Silver.

"No," said the captain.

"Who'll give me a hand up?" roared Silver.

Not a man among us moved. Long John Silver crawled along the sand until he reached his crutch. Then he spat on the ground.

"There," he cried, "that's what I think of ye all! Before the hour's out, them that die will be the lucky ones!"

He stumbled, swearing, to the fence. His mates helped him over and he disappeared into the trees.

"To your posts!" cried Captain Smollett, "we're outnumbered, I needn't tell you that. But we can win."

We took our guns and powder and scattered. Suddenly, with a loud roar, a little cloud of pirates leaped from the woods on the north side, and ran straight to the stockade. At the same time, a small rifle ball came from the woods, straight into the stockade, and blew the doctor's gun to pieces.

The pirates swung over the fence like monkeys. Five men fell, though one was more frightened than hurt, and he got up again and ran back to the trees. Other men in the woods fired at us all the time. Four pirates ran up the hill and jumped on us.

I picked up a sword and ran outside into the sunlight.

"Round behind the house, lads!" called the captain, "round the house!"

I ran round the corner of the cabin and found myself face to face with one of the pirates. He roared and lifted his sword. I had no time to be afraid. I leaped to one side, fell in the sand and rolled down the slope.

As I climbed back up, I could see that five of the pirates were dead or injured.

"Fire — fire from the house!" cried the doctor. "And you, lad, take cover!"

No shots had to be fired. The pirates ran off into the woods. But one of our men was dead and two, including the captain, were wounded.

"They won't be back today," cried the captain. "And now we're four against nine! That's better odds. We were seven to nineteen at the start."

After we had eaten, when the sun was overhead, I saw the doctor whispering to the squire. Then he picked up his hat, pistol, dagger and the map, and walked quickly towards the woods.

"If I'm right," I thought, "he's going to see Ben Gunn."

I could not bear the heat inside the stockade, or the waiting. I picked up some biscuits and my pistols and crept outside. I was going to do something foolish, I knew that. I would take a walk to cool my head, and at the same time, find out if Ben Gunn *did* keep his boat under the white rock.

CHAPTER SEVEN

Out to sea

I made my way straight to the east coast of the island. It was warm and sunny although it was late in the afternoon. A cool breeze began to reach me as I caught sight of the sea. I made my way carefully under cover of the bushes.

Suddenly, I was looking down on the *Hispaniola*.

Although the ship was nearly a mile away, I recognised Long John Silver at once. He was in one of the small boats, laughing and talking to his men on the ship. A loud scream made me jump and I got ready to run. I heard another scream. But it was only Captain Flint, perched on his master's wrist, screeching to be heard.

The sun was sinking fast behind Spy-Glass Hill as I watched, and a thick fog began to come down. I set off again. I *had* to find the boat before dark. Night had almost come when I reached the white rock. And there it was – Ben Gunn's boat.

I should have gone straight back to the stockade; but a new idea had been growing in my head for some time.

"Now that I have a boat, I could go out to the *Hispaniola* and cut her anchor," I told myself.

I sat down and waited for darkness. It was the perfect

night for my plan. The fog hid everything. I could see only two things – the pirates' fire on the beach, and the light from the ship.

I pushed the boat in the water. It was hard to handle and I floated everywhere, except the way I wanted to go. By good luck, the tide took me straight for the ship. She loomed up in front of me, blacker than darkness.

"I cannot cut her anchor now," I sighed, "the rope is too tight. It will spring back and knock me straight out of the water."

I waited. A puff of wind caught the ship and turned her, loosening the anchor rope for a moment. I cut it.

The boat was swept against the side of the ship. I pushed hard until I was clear of it; but at the last moment, I saw a fine rope hanging from the ship. I don't know why I did what I did. I suppose I was curious. I suddenly wanted to look inside the cabin window. So I grasped the rope and swung past the window. In the smoky lamp light, I saw Israel Hands and another pirate called O'Brien with their hands around each other's throats.

I jumped back into my little boat. Suddenly, she lurched under me and she seemed to change course. I glanced over my shoulder and my heart jumped against my ribs. There, *behind* me, was the glow of the camp fire. We were heading out to sea!

I lay down in the bottom of my little boat and prepared to die. I lay there for hours, tossed backwards and forwards by the waves and expecting to be thrown into the sea at every wave. At last I fell asleep and dreamed of home. It was daylight when I woke up. Mizzen-Mast Hill, bare and dark rose behind tall cliffs, on the south-west coast of Treasure Island.

"I can easily get ashore from here," I said to myself. "It's only about a mile."

I paddled hard with my hands, but I could not get very close. The rocks were too tall and the waves were too rough. I was also frightened of the strange animals on the rocks, huge slimy monsters like huge snails. I know now that they were harmless sea-lions.

"I'll make for the Cape of the Woods," I muttered. "I saw it marked on the map. There's a long stretch of sand there at low tide, and plenty of trees to hide me."

The sea was smoother now and a gentle wind blew from the south. I was very thirsty and my throat burned with the salt-water. I came closer and closer to the shore and I could even see the tree tops swaying in the breeze; but the current carried me past the cape, towards the open sea again.

I groaned. Then a moment later, I gasped in surprise.

Right in front of me was the *Hispaniola*.

"She's in full sail, "I thought. "They must be going back to the island to fetch the others. I don't care if they capture me now, I must have water to drink."

I stared at the ship for some time.

"She isn't sailing smoothly," I thought. "There's nobody steering her. If I got on board, I could take her back to Captain Smollett! I'm ready for another little adventure."

I paddled as fast as I could, only stopping to bale out water. Soon, I was alongside the ship. There was no one on deck. The wind fell for a moment and the *Hispaniola* turned round slowly, bringing her alongside me. This was my only chance. As I came up on the next wave, I jumped into the air and caught hold of the bow of the ship and hung there.

I heard a thud below me and I knew that my little boat had been crushed.

There was no going back now.

CHAPTER EIGHT

On the pirate ship

I flung myself onto the top deck. Suddenly the wind blew the sail hard and I could see the main deck below. Two men lay there – O'Brien with his arms stretched out, and Israel Hands sitting up with his head on his chest, his face as white as a candle. There were splashes of dark blood on the planks.

Israel Hands suddenly moved and gave a low moan. I felt sorry for him until I remembered that he was one of Silver's mutineers.

"Brandy," he muttered.

I went down into the cabin. The lamp was still burning. The floor was thick with mud, there were dirty fingermarks everywhere. Every lock had been broken in the search for the treasure map. I took a long drink of water before going back up on deck. I gave Hands his brandy.

"He's good and dead," he muttered, pointing to O'Brien.

"Well," I said, "I've come aboard to take back this ship. And you, Mr. Hands, shall look upon me as your captain from now on."

I ran to the mast and took down the pirate flag and

threw it into the sea.

"God save the King!" I shouted, "and there's an end to Captain Silver!"

I went back to Hands.

"I'm going to take her back to Treasure Island," I told him.

"If you gives me food and drink, and an old scarf to tie my wound up," whispered Hands, "I'll tell you how to sail her in."

I agreed. We skimmed before the breeze, like a bird, towards the island. I had plenty to eat and drink. But I was worried by the odd look on Hands' face as he watched me work.

"This brandy's too strong for my head," he said. "You get me a bottle of wine, Jim."

I didn't believe him. I went towards the cabin, took off my shoes and crept back to the top deck where I could look down on Hands. He was crawling across the deck to a pile of rope. He picked out a blood-stained dagger and hid it in his jacket. Then he crawled back to his place.

"He is armed and he can move about. That's all I need to know," I thought. "But we both want the ship back on the island. I shall be safe until then."

I was right. As soon as the *Hispaniola* had run onto the shore, I heard a noise behind me. I turned round. Hands was already there, the dagger in his hand. We both cried out when our eyes met – his a cry of anger, mine a cry of terror. He threw himself at me and I leaped sideways. I had to let the steering tiller go and it knocked Hands over.

I took out my pistol and fired at him. There was no sound, no fire. The sea water had wet my gunpowder! I ran to the mast and dodged him again and again. I had often played this game at home on the rocks of Black Hill Cove. But how long could I hold out?

Suddenly, the *Hispaniola* leaned over in the soft sand. We rolled over, and O'Brien's dead body rolled after us. I got up first and climbed up the mast. Now I had time to put fresh powder into my pistols. Hands started to climb up after me, the dagger in his mouth.

"One more step, Mr. Hands," I said, "and I'll blow your brains out!"

He stopped and took the dagger from his mouth. He started to speak and I was sure that he would go down again. But he threw his dagger at me. I felt a blow, then a sharp pain, and there I was pinned by the shoulder to the mast. And in my surprise, I fired both pistols. With a cry, Israel Hands plunged head-first into the water. He rose once to the surface and sank for good, shot and drowned.

I felt sick, faint and terrified. Hot blood was running

over my back and chest. The dagger burned my shoulder
like a hot iron. I shivered violently, and in doing so, my
skin broke away from the dagger. I climbed down the
mast and tied up my wound.

I could not bear the sight of O'Brien. I dragged him
like a sack of flour and threw him overboard. His red cap

came off and floated on the water. I looked down. I could see him and Israel lying side by side, and fish swimming over them.

The sun was just beginning to set and an evening breeze had started to blow. I jumped overboard onto the sand.

"I have not come back empty-handed," I thought as I looked at the *Hispaniola* in front of me, "there she is, ready for our own men to board and take to sea again. I cannot wait to tell them of my adventures."

I made my way to the stockade by the light of a full moon. As I came close, I went more carefully. The far end of the cabin was still in deep darkness. At the other end were the remains of a fire. I stopped, afraid.

"We never built big fires like that," I thought.

I crept into the shadows and crawled towards the corner of the cabin. I almost laughed as I heard the sound of snoring!

"All's well!" I thought happily.

I walked inside.

"Pieces of eight! Pieces of eight!" cried a shrill voice.

Then I heard Silver himself.

"Who goes?" he shouted.

I turned to run, but someone caught hold of me. My worst fear had come true: Long John Silver and his pirates had broken through the stockade.

CHAPTER NINE
In the pirate camp

I stared at Silver in the light of the flaming torch.

"So," he said, "here's Jim Hawkins, shiver my timbers! Dropped in to see us, eh? Well, I call that friendly!"

He stopped to light his pipe.

"Now, Jim," he said, "I've always liked you, I have, for a lad of spirit. Just like myself when I was young and handsome. You'll have to join my men. You can't go back to your own, they won't have you."

"Where are they?" I asked. "What are *you* doing here?"

"I don't know, Mr. Hawkins," Silver said. "Yesterday morning, the doctor came down to talk to us. He told me the old ship was gone and that he and the others wanted to leave the stockade."

"And here you all are, in a bad way!" I cried. "Ship lost, treasure lost, men lost! And if you want to know who did it – it was I! *I* was in the apple barrel the night we saw land. I heard every word. *I* cut the ship's cable, I killed the men aboard, and it was I who brought her here, but you'll never find her. I no more fear you than I fear a fly. Kill me, if you please. But if you don't, I'll speak for you in court when you're tried for piracy."

I stopped, out of breath. Not a man moved, but they all stared at me like sheep. Then one of them drew out his knife. I stood straight against the wall, my heart pounding.

"I like this boy!" roared Silver. "He's more a man than any pair of rats in this here house. And don't you forget, *I'm* the captain here."

"We'll need to talk about that," said the man.

He went outside, and, one by one, the others followed him.

"Now, look you here, Jim Hawkins," Silver said quietly, "I'll save your life – from them – if you save Long John from hanging. I know you've got that ship safe somewhere."

Silver's men talked around the fire for some time and it burned low before they came back. I could see the moon shining on their knives.

"Here they come," I said to Silver.

And I stood against the wall and waited.

"Let them come, lad – let 'em come," said Silver cheerily, "I've still got my pistol."

The door of the cabin opened and the five men stood together, then they pushed one man forward. He put out his closed right hand and slipped something into Silver's hand.

"The black spot! I thought so," said Silver, looking at the piece of paper in his hand.

"Just you turn it over, and see what's wrote there," said the pirate.

"*Stand down*," read Silver. "No, I won't. I'm still your captain till you tells me what's wrong."

"You made a mess of this cruise," said the man, "*and you let the doctor go*."

"You listen to me!" roared Silver. "Here's why!"

He threw a piece of paper onto the floor that I recognised at once. It was the map of Treasure Island! I could hardly believe my eyes. Why had the doctor given it to him?

The pirates leaped on the map like cats on a mouse. They laughed like children.

"Silver!" they cried. "Barbecue for ever! Barbecue for captain! And tomorrow, we hunt for treasure!"

CHAPTER TEN

The treasure hunt

We were a strange sight as we set off that morning. Six of us all in dirty sailor clothes, all carrying pistols except me. *I* was led on a rope like a dancing bear. On the way, the men read out the directions from the map.

> *"Tall tree, Spy-glass shoulder,*
> *compass point N. of NNE.*
> *Skeleton Island ESE and by E*
> *Ten feet."*

We headed for Spy-Glass Hill and started to climb the slope to the top where we could see tall pine trees. As we came nearer, one of the men on the left gave a piercing scream. Then, terrified, he screamed again, and pointed to the ground. We ran towards him and looked down. In front of us lay a human skeleton, pointing in the direction of Skeleton Island.

"This is one of Captain Flint's jokes," said Silver. "It makes me cold inside to think of him. He killed every one of those six men – and he dragged this one here to point the way. Aye, six they were, and six are we. And bones is what they are now."

We set off again. But in spite of the hot sun, we kept side by side, whispering, terrified of a dead pirate. Above us rose the Spy-Glass.

Silver took out his compass.

"There are three tall trees," he said, "in a line from Skeleton Island. "*Shoulder*" is that low point there. It's child's play to find the treasure now. Come on."

Suddenly, out of the trees in front of us, came a thin, high, trembling voice.

"Fifteen men on the dead man's chest
Yo-ho-ho, and a bottle of rum!"

The pirates turned deathly white and held on to each other.

"It's Flint!" one of them shouted.

The song stopped. Then the voice began to wail.

"Fetch the rum, Darby!"

"They were Flint's last words," gasped another, "before he died."

"Shipmates!" cried Silver, "I'm here to get that treasure. I was never afraid of Flint in his life and I'll face him dead."

He paused for a moment.

"I know that voice," he roared angrily, "It's Ben Gunn!"

"Why, nobody minds Ben Gunn!" cried one of the men, "dead or alive, nobody minds him."

It was amazing how the men's high spirits returned. We set off again, with Silver's compass to keep us on the right line with Skeleton Island. The pines grew wide apart as we came near to the slope of the Spy Glass. We reached the tallest, and the thought of that treasure buried under its spreading shadows took away everybody's terror. The men began to run forward.

Silver had a glint in his eyes and I knew he was thinking only of himself. I thought of Flint's men, murdered here. I could hear their cries and I shivered.

Suddenly, the men stopped. A cry rose up from them. Silver hobbled forward as quickly as he could, almost pulling me over. Then we, too, stopped and stared.

In front of us was an enormous hole, empty except for the broken planks from a sea-chest, branded with one word – WALRUS.

…I can still see the look of fear on Silver's face as he handed me a pistol. But we didn't have to fight. Ben Gunn, the doctor and the squire were hiding in the woods. They killed two of the pirates and the others ran away.

Why hadn't I listened to Ben Gunn that day in the woods when he told me he was rich? He had already dug up the treasure, and told Dr. Livesey. At last I understood why the doctor had given the map to Silver.

We left Treasure Island with Ben Gunn as soon as we could load the treasure from his cabin. On the way to England, Long John Silver stole one of the small boats and a bag of gold. We were pleased to be rid of him.

I would never go back to that island, even though there is more treasure there. Now that I am back in England, back with my mother at the Inn, I sometimes wake up in the middle of the night, trembling with fear, with the sharp voice of Long John Silver's parrot ringing in my ears:

"Pieces of eight! Pieces of eight!"